Princess Florizella

Princess Florizella is an extremely unusual princess!

She wears patched jeans, and she climbs trees. She rides her horse Jellybean, and she goes on picnics. She doesn't care how she looks, and worst of all for her parents who wanted an ordinary fairy-tale princess, she won't be rescued by anybody, and she won't get married.

A funny story featuring the most unusual princess in fairy-tale land.

Philippa Gregory is best known for her novels for adults; this is her first children's story. She holds a doctorate from the University of Edinburgh for her research into eighteenth-century literature. She trained as a journalist working for newspapers and BBC radio. She teaches in adult education and is a founder-member of a community centre for unemployed people in the North East of England where she lives with her daughter. Her best-selling novels, *Wideacre* and *The Favoured Child* are the first two parts of a trilogy about a family in eighteenth-century Sussex.

By the same author

WIDEACRE

THE FAVOURED CHILD

published by Viking and Penguin.

OCHRE PARK IMC

PHILIPPA GREGORY

PRINCESS FLORIZELLA

ILLUSTRATED BY ALISON CLAIRE DARKE

PUFFIN BOOKS

PUFFIN BOOKS

Published by the Penguin Group
27 Wrights Lane, London W8 5TZ, England
Viking Penguin Inc., 40 West 23rd Street, New York, New York 10010, USA
Penguin Books Australia Ltd, Ringwood, Victoria, Australia
Penguin Books Canada Ltd, 2801 John Street, Markham, Ontario, Canada L3R 1B4
Penguin Books (NZ) Ltd, 182–190 Wairau Road, Auckland 10, New Zealand

Penguin Books Ltd, Registered Offices: Harmondsworth, Middlesex, England

First published by Viking Kestrel 1988
Published in Puffin Books 1989
10 9 8 7 6 5 4 3 2 1

Made and printed in Great Britain by
Richard Clay Ltd, Bungay, Suffolk
Filmset in Linotron Palatino

For Victoria

Princess Florizella

Once upon a time (that means I don't exactly know when, but it wasn't that long ago), in the Seven Kingdoms, the King and Queen very much wanted a son. They waited and they waited until one day the Queen told her husband, "I have a surprise for you. We are going to have a beautiful baby boy!"

But when the baby came, it was a surprise to both of them.

For it was not a boy. It was a girl.

She was the ugliest baby anyone had ever seen.

Not all babies are beautiful, though they all need loving. Some are noisy and some of them are sad. They are the ones that need loving most of all. Florizella was not a sad one. She was a happy one. But she was most dreadfully ugly.

She had no hair, no hair at all. Her face was red as a mashed strawberry.

Her nose was a podgy little button, and her eyes were tiny piggy ones. Worse than that, she had spots! Worse than *that*, she kept being sick!

It was a big surprise to the King and Queen, I can tell you.

But they loved her all the same. Just as much as if she had been beautiful.

(If you were only loved if you were pretty, hippos would never have babies at all, would they?)

As Princess Florizella grew up, she became no prettier. But people soon stopped noticing. She was such a mischievous, making-a-noise-and-running-away little girl that they spent half their time telling her that she would be in Big Trouble and the other half making excuses for her, and they wasted no time at all on how she looked. How she behaved was enough for anyone!

The King and Queen had been so sure that they were going to have a beautiful baby boy that, even though they loved Florizella, for a while they managed to make themselves feel quite sad. But the picture in their minds of the Prince who never was became fainter and fainter every day, and pretty soon it disappeared altogether.

By the time Florizella was fifteen no one would have wanted her any different if they'd had the choice. (And, since they didn't have the choice, that was just as well.)

As for Florizella, she never troubled her head about what anyone thought. She didn't care how she looked either. She knew some pretty girls – of course she did. Some very pretty girls were friends of hers, and Florizella thought their hair was nice and their clothes were nice and their shoes were nice. But, oh, their days would have bored her to death in a week!

In the morning they got up, washed their faces and put cream on their cheeks and on their hands and on their noses. Then it was time for

breakfast. They didn't eat too much in case they got fat, and they didn't eat anything fried in case it gave them spots. They got dressed and that took them an hour, and then they did their hair and *that* took until lunch-time. By the time the afternoon came they were too tired to do anything but pluck their eyebrows.

Meanwhile Florizella, who wasn't interested in trying to be pretty, jumped out of bed in the mornings, had a quick wash, pulled on her jeans and went horse-riding. She had a wonderful horse called Jellybean, and she galloped him just about everywhere.

When Florizella had ridden enough, she came home and worked with her mother and her father in the Royal Office. She was going to be Queen one day, and she warned them that she would be making changes.

She said that she wouldn't live on her own in the palace.

Florizella thought that everyone should live in the size of house that they needed. So families with lots of babies or who had friends living with them should have the biggest houses, and small families should have the smallest houses.

"That sounds rather sensible," said the Queen, who was sick of dusting.

Florizella had other ideas too.

She thought that everyone should

be paid money whether they went out to work or not. Then fathers who wanted to stay at home and look after the children could do so. And when mothers went out to work, they could come home to a clean, tidy house.

"It would never work," said the King, who didn't like dusting either.

One way and another Florizella had a lot of ideas about how she would change the Seven Kingdoms when they were hers. In the meantime she rode her horse, read lots of books and swung on her swing. Sometimes she thought her parents were Horrid, and sometimes she thought they were Lovely! Most of the time she just got on with the important business of growing up.

One day an invitation came to the palace. It said "Princess Florizella" on the front in wonderful curly writing. It was an invitation for a ball given by Prince Bennett in the next-door Kingdom. He wanted to choose a Princess to marry.

"I'd like to go," said Princess

Florizella at breakfast when the invitation arrived.

The King looked at the Queen with a grown-up look which meant that she must start the job of telling Florizella "No".

"I don't think you'd enjoy it," she said nicely.

Florizella said she thought she would.

"There would be so many people there," the Queen said.

Florizella said that she didn't mind that.

"You'll have to spend the night away from home."

Florizella looked a bit surprised and asked what on earth was wrong with that?

The Queen gave the King "That Look" back, and he said, rather impatiently, for he was uncomfortable when he thought he might hurt Florizella's feelings:

"The thing is, Florizella, Prince Bennett will never choose you to be his bride because there will be very, very pretty Princesses there, behaving like pretty Princesses should. And you have never been like that. Not at all."

"I know that," said Florizella, smiling. "But I'm not going there to get married to Prince Bennett. I'm going to see all the other people and enjoy the party."

Then the King and Queen waggled their eyebrows at each other in a

whole exchange of grown-up looks,
and then they said Florizella could
certainly go. So she threw a clean pair
of jeans in a bag, and after lunch she
hopped into the carriage – for they
had no cars and trains or buses in the
Seven Kingdoms then – and drove off
with her horse, Jellybean, following
behind.

Prince Bennett's Kingdom was not very far from Florizella's home, and Florizella was the first to arrive. The Prince had invited one hundred and twenty-one Princesses, and Florizella waited at the gate to see them all drive by. One hundred and twenty Princesses went by, some in fine carriages, some in smaller ones, and one or two in carts! Some of them were very beautiful and some were less so; but they all wanted to marry Prince Bennett. They didn't have anything else to do, you see. Only Princess One Hundred and Twenty-One, Florizella, was not planning marriage. She was just there to see the fun.

"And eat the food!" said Princess

Florizella, longingly, when she saw
the banquet.

She had a wonderful time. There
were all sorts of meats and every kind
of sandwich. There were tons of

cakes, even the ones with little chocolate buttons on the top. There were three hundred different sorts of ice-cream and forty different coloured jellies. There were pizzas and beans and hot-dogs. There was candy-floss and sticks of rock. There were toffee apples and peppermint creams. Everything that is best to eat, and that normally you're not allowed, was there. Florizella ate far too much of it, and nobody minded at all.

But the one hundred and twenty Princesses ate a little bread and butter and nothing more.

They were worried about spilling things on their best ballgowns.

They were worried about whether they would be able to dance lightly on their toes if they ate as much as they wanted.

They were worried that someone might be watching them and think that they were greedy.

Princess Florizella worried about nothing. She ate like she was half-starved. She had seconds and thirds of nearly everything.

Not even Prince Bennett ate as much as her. He had to dance with every single one of the one hundred and twenty-one Princesses, and he thought he had better make an early start. He danced with each Princess, one after another, and they all smiled and agreed with whatever he said.

They were lovely. They were the nicest girls he had ever met. They were so pleasant he could not tell them apart. And they were so kind and charming to him that he had the horrid feeling that nobody could be that nice *all* the time. So how could he possibly find out which of them were nice for most of the time? One or two might not be nice at all, but might just be putting it on for the party. And very sorry he would be if he married one of them! Prince Bennett's head was spinning by the time he came and sat down beside Florizella, who was just finishing a bowl of strawberries and cream.

"Would you like a dance?" he asked, politely.

"Not especially," said Florizella. "And I would have thought you might have had enough dancing for one evening."

Prince Bennett jumped in surprise. "Yes, I have," he said, honestly. "I think it's the horridest party that ever was."

"Have a choc-ice," said Florizella to cheer him up, and Prince Bennett started to feel better.

"You're a girl." he said, trustingly. "You tell me. How can you tell which Princesses are really nice and which are just pretending?"

Florizella thought for a moment. "I don't know them any better than you

do," she said. "They certainly all *seem* very nice."

"That's just it!" Bennett groaned. "I *cannot* choose which one to marry."

"Don't marry any of 'em then," Florizella said, helpfully. "Don't marry anyone. I wouldn't."

"But I have to!" Prince Bennett exclaimed. "All Princes have to give balls and choose their Princess and get married. Then they have to live happily ever after."

Florizella frowned. "It's a bit of a chance, though, isn't it?" she said.

Prince Bennett nodded. "I know," he said dolefully.

Then the band played, and poor Prince Bennett had to go and dance with another Princess and then another one until the ball had ended. Florizella had a dance with him later on, which she enjoyed, even though he trod on her toes.

That night all the beautiful Princesses set their alarm clocks for six in the morning to give themselves time to have their baths, wash their hair and put on new dresses for breakfast. Prince Bennett was in the breakfast parlour waiting for them, and as each Princess came in, he bowed very low and said:

"Good morning!"

Each Princess curtsied and smiled, and said:

"Good morning, Prince Bennett!"

Then the tired Prince said:

"What would you like for breakfast?"

And each Princess said:

"I don't know. What are *you* having?"

When Prince Bennett said he was having bacon and eggs, every one of the one hundred and twenty Princesses gasped as if he had said something dreadful, and said:

"Oh, no! Not for me! Just toast, please!"

So he was very glad to see Princess Florizella, who came in late because she had been out to the stables to see her horse. And he was very glad when she said at once that she would

like bacon and eggs and tomatoes and
sausages too if they had any. They
had a most peaceful, hearty breakfast
while, all around, the one hundred
and twenty Princesses crunched toast
and looked thin and beautiful.

After breakfast, Prince Bennett
asked the Princess on his right what
she would like to do that day. And the
Princess on his right said:

"I don't know. What would *you* like to do?"

Then Prince Bennett asked the Princess on his left what she would like to do that day. And she said:

"I don't know. What would *you* like to do?"

Then Princess Florizella said, nicely, to them all:

"Why don't we all ride down to the river and go swimming? We could take a picnic with us."

Well – some of the Princesses couldn't ride, and some of them couldn't swim. Some of them hadn't got trousers for riding, and some of them hadn't got swimming costumes. Some of them were frightened of cold water, and some of them were frightened of horses. In the end, no one went . . . except Princess Florizella and Prince Bennett.

They had a lovely day.

When they were trotting back to the Prince's palace in the evening, just as the stars were starting to come out and the sky was getting grey, Prince Bennett said, happily:

"Florizella, I've had a wonderful idea. I won't marry any of the one hundred and twenty beautiful Princesses. I'll marry you!"

And then Florizella said something which surprised him so much that he nearly fell off his horse.

"No, thank you," she said, politely.

Prince Bennett gawped at her.

"Why ever not?" he asked.

"Look here," said Florizella, reasonably, "I told you I wasn't going to marry, and I meant it. One day I shall inherit the Seven Kingdoms, and there are a lot of things I want to do there. I don't want to come and be your Queen. I'm not even sure that I think Kings and Queens are a good idea. It might be a lot better for everyone if people made up their own laws and didn't have one person bossing them around.

"I don't want to come and live in your palace. I've got a perfectly good palace of my own, and I'm not planning to keep that one all to myself. Another home would just be greedy.

"I don't want to live in your country. I've got one of my own. I don't need your fortune. I can earn my own money. I'd very much like it if you were my friend, my best friend if you like. But I don't want to marry you. I'm not going to marry anyone for a good long time."

Prince Bennett rode along saying nothing for a little while. But then he smiled.

"Florizella," he said, "I think I agree with you. I don't think I shall marry for a while either. I shall tell my mother and father. And I should like to be best friends with you."

So Princess Florizella and Prince Bennett shook hands and rode back, side by side, in the starlight.

After the Ball

When Florizella got home the King
and Queen were waiting for her at the
door of the palace.

"How did you get on?" asked the
Queen.

"Who did he choose for his bride?"
asked the King.

"How many Princesses were there
at the ball?" asked the Queen.

"Did you see the Princess of Three
Rivers?" the King asked.

Florizella laughed and jumped out
of the carriage.

"I had a lovely time," she said.

"And he decided in the end not to marry anybody. There were one hundred and twenty Princesses there as well as me, and I didn't spot the Princess of the Three Rivers, but the place was so awash with Princesses that I didn't even see the Princess of the Two Mountains, who should have been there."

"Not marrying!" said the King.

"Not marrying!" said the Queen.

Then they both fell on Florizella at once, demanding to know what on earth could have happened if a royal Prince should give a Princess-choosing ball and then choose none of them.

So Florizella explained that Prince Bennett thought that the nice

Princesses might have been just acting nice and might be secretly rather awful to live with, and that he hadn't wanted to take the chance.

"Did he ask no one at all then?" demanded the King.

"Oh, yes," said Florizella. "He asked me. But I told him I didn't want to marry yet."

The King and Queen gaped at each other as if they could not believe their ears. Then they both rushed at Florizella and made her sit down and tell them all about the ball and the breakfast and the horse-ride and Prince Bennett asking her to marry him. Then the King jumped to his feet and went to the window and said, "Well, well, well," a great many times, very softly.

And the Queen had a little smile on her face as she looked at Florizella.

"What a match!" said the King. "Prince Bennett's Kingdom was beyond my wildest hopes!"

"What a triumph!" said the Queen. "And everyone always said she was such an *odd* sort of Princess!"

Florizella looked from one to the other.

"I said I didn't want to marry him, and we agreed to be just friends," she said.

But they weren't listening. They had Ideas in their heads, and the Ideas and Florizella were all jumbled up.

And nothing she could say to either of them could stop them and their Ideas.

The first day, her father, the King, laughed and teased her. The second day, the Queen spoke of inviting Prince Bennett over to stay. The next couple of days there were lots of letters between Prince Bennett's parents and Florizella's mother and father. Then on the fifth day the King told Florizella outright that she was to marry Bennett whether she wanted to or not.

Florizella looked at him as if he were crazy.

"You can't make me marry someone if I don't want to," she said. "And I told you that I didn't want to."

"Oh, can't I?" said the King, who was not always in Perfect Control of

his temper. He snatched Florizella up and bundled her upstairs as if he were some dreadful father out of a story-book. I am not at all sorry to say that Florizella bit *and* scratched *and* shouted back at him when he locked her in her bedroom.

"You'll stay there until you agree to marry Prince Bennett!" he bawled through the keyhole.

"Nonsense," said Florizella, who had no time for men who tried to boss her about. She knew perfectly well that her father had no right to lock her up, or to order her to marry anyone. She also knew if she wanted to leave, then nothing was easier than to open her bedroom window and shin down the drainpipe. She got out of the castle most mornings like that when she went horse-riding. It was easier than opening the great double doors and raising the portcullis on her own. But, instead of running off, she thought she would wait until her father came to let her out and talk the whole thing over with him.

"I'm not standing for this," said Florizella to herself. "But he'll come round sooner or later." And she got one of her favourite story-books and settled down for a quiet morning's reading.

It looked as if it might be later rather than sooner, for Florizella's lunch came up on a tray. At tea-time they sent up a cup of tea and a slice of cake,

and by dinner-time Florizella had
finished her book and was pretty
bored with spending all day indoors.
At bed-time her father came to the
door and said in his most kingly voice:

"My daughter, Princess Florizella,
are you ready to agree to marry Prince
Bennett now?"

Florizella, who was rather sulky for she had wasted a whole day indoors while the sun was shining outside and the birds were singing and the grass was growing, said:

"Certainly not! And you know you shouldn't treat a daughter like this. Not even in a fairy story."

At that the King stamped off to bed

in a terrible temper. He was cross
because Florizella would not do as he
wanted, and he was cross because he
knew perfectly well he was in the
wrong, in spite of being a King and
quite grown-up.

"Well, you're not acting grown-up
at all," said the Queen, grumpily, to
him. "And tomorrow Florizella is to be
let out, whatever she says about
Prince Bennett."

The King said, "Humph," as if he
meant "No". But he really meant
"Yes". He'd had enough of being cross
anyway.

But next morning, before anyone was
up, there was a great *Tooroo! Tooroo!* at
the palace gates, and in galloped

Prince Bennett with half a dozen of his courtiers, a dozen soldiers and a couple of trumpeters. Just an informal visit.

He had come to see the King, for someone had told him that Princess Florizella was locked up in her room and that the King would not let her out until she promised to marry the Prince.

Prince Bennett popped up to the

King's bedroom and argued with him while the King sat up in bed and scowled and wanted his morning tea. He had never liked Bennett less than he did at that moment.

"Fancy having him in the palace!" the King thought crossly to himself. "Never a peaceful morning."

But out loud all he said was that Prince Bennett should go home and wait for a message, and that he was

49

certain that Florizella would agree to marry him in the near future. And then his cup of tea arrived, and he looked so hard at the door and at Prince Bennett that even Bennett could see that he was very much in the way. There was nothing to do but to make a bow and get himself out of the room as quickly as he could go backwards. (You're not supposed to turn your back on the Royals. It's another one of those rules which makes life especially difficult when you have monarchs around.)

Prince Bennett didn't go home. He popped round to the back of the castle and called like an owl until Princess Florizella put her head out of the window and said:

"Don't be silly, Bennett, everyone knows you don't have owls in daylight. Besides, you don't sound much like an owl to me."

Then they argued about whether or not owls made calls like too-wit-too-whoo. (Actually they don't. It's more like whoo-whoo.) They made owl calls at each other until all the windows opened and lots of people put their heads out to see what was going on.

"What is that awful noise?" the Queen asked her maid, who was brushing the royal wig.

"Princess Florizella's young Prince is making signals to her," said the maid, leaning out of the window to have a look.

"He's come to rescue her, then,"

said the Queen, extremely pleased. "That's very prompt. I like a young man who gets on with a rescue. When I was a Princess, my future husband, the King, was late. I was tied to a rock for three days, and if the sea-monster had not had an upset stomach that day, he might have been too late altogether. It's not all fun being a Princess, you know."

The maid nodded and looked out of the window again.

"He's climbing up to her bedroom," she said.

"That's unusual," said the Queen, interested. "I'd have thought Florizella would have had the sheets knotted together by now. Not like her to be slow. How is he climbing? Not

by her hair – her hair isn't long
enough. She *will* keep having it cut. I
told her she'd need it long one of these
days."

"Up the ivy, Ma'am," said the maid.
"Looks a bit unsteady to me."

The Queen smiled because it had
been her idea to plant the ivy outside
Princess Florizella's bedroom on the
morning she was born, just to be
ready for this very occasion. And now
here was Prince Bennett climbing up
to Florizella! It was very gratifying.
Next, Bennett would rescue Florizella
and ride away with her. Then she and
the King could forgive them and they
could all have a wonderful party and
live happily ever after.

But she should have remembered

that Florizella was not like other Princesses.

Prince Bennett should have remembered that Florizella was not like other Princesses.

She was not a bit grateful to him for climbing up the ivy.

Actually, she was rather cross.

"But I've come to rescue you!" Bennett protested.

"How did you get up to my bedroom window?" she demanded,

as if she had not seen him scrambling up and grabbing for a drainpipe when a branch broke.

"Up the ivy," Bennett said, surprised. "You know I did, you saw me climbing!"

"And don't you think," said Florizella, sarcastically, "that if *you* can climb up, then *I* can perfectly well climb down?"

Bennett said nothing. He hadn't thought of that. He was so used to the old idea of Princesses who sat still and waited to be rescued that he had forgotten that Florizella was not that sort of Princess.

"Now go," said Florizella, giving him a little push towards the window. "It's bad enough with everyone

nagging me to marry you, without
you looking like a Prince in an old
fairy story as well."

"But what about you?" Bennett
asked, rather worried.

Florizella laughed. "My father will
let me out soon enough," she said.

"And if I get too bored, I can always climb down the ivy and go for a ride. When I'm out, I'll come over and see you. But I'll stay here for now. My father shouldn't have locked me in, and I want to talk it over with him. He'll never learn to treat girls properly unless someone tells him how."

Bennett thought that perhaps Florizella was not a very comfortable daughter for anyone to have. And he thought that perhaps she would not be a very comfortable wife. But she was a jolly nice friend. So he shook hands with her and climbed down the ivy again.

"Gracious me, Ma'am!" squawked the Queen's maid. "It's Prince Bennett climbing down the ivy again. On his own! He's left the Princess behind!"

The Queen dashed to the window and watched Prince Bennett scramble down.

"Oh, no!" she said. "Oh, no! Oh, Florizella!"

When the King heard what had happened he went bananas.

There was no chance that Florizella was going to be let out now!

He had been so sure that Bennett was going to rescue her, he was even prepared to overlook the way the Prince had bothered him so early in the morning. But to go without taking Princess Florizella with him!

"Absolutely unreasonable!" he said and stumped off to the garden to prune the roses. You wouldn't have

wanted to be a rose in the garden of the Seven Kingdoms on that day, I can tell you. It was a massacre! There wasn't a single rose left standing by lunch-time. But the King was feeling a lot better.

Until the messenger came, that is.

It was one of Prince Bennett's trumpeters. She came *tooroo, tooroo*ing into the courtyard in a terrible hurry, scaring the hens half to death and setting the guard dogs barking.

"Prince Bennett has been captured!" she shouted. "Captured by a dragon in the Purple Forest!"

Everyone came running at once, Florizella leaned as far as she could out of the window to hear. The messenger told them that the great two-headed dragon had jumped out at the Prince and his courtiers and that everyone had ridden away as fast as they could except for Prince Bennett, whose horse had reared and dropped him right at the dragon's feet. Bennett had bent his sword in the fall and couldn't draw it from the scabbard! The dragon had picked him up and tied him to a tree, using all sorts of difficult knots, and was sitting beside him, waiting (as is only fair and proper) for the rescue party to arrive within forty-eight hours before eating the Prince up – every little bit of him except, possibly, the bent sword.

"Ooo-er!" said Florizella on hearing this, and she leaned out of the window and whistled a loud, clear

whistle which Jellybean could hear
wherever he happened to be. He was
in his stable and had to back up
against the far wall and take a little
run at the door and rear up and jump
over it, and then he came galloping

around and stood under Florizella's window, while Florizella grabbed her sword and her dagger and a spare sword for Prince Bennett (which she kept in the wardrobe in the space for the long dresses) and shinned down the ivy as quickly as she could – which was very quick indeed!

Then she dropped from the last branch on to Jellybean's back and galloped as fast as she could to the Purple Forest, steering Jellybean with the halter rope and clinging on tight to the swords.

She saw the dragon before he saw her.

He had dozed off while he was waiting, but he had put an alarm clock in one of his great green ears to wake him when the forty-eight hours were up. His great snores bent the tallest trees of the Purple Forest and made a noise like a thousand thunderstorms. And his horrid, smoky breath had scorched all the grass and flowers and bushes for three miles all around so

that Jellybean snorted and shivered at the dreadful smell of burning.

Bennett was tied to a tree with fiendishly complicated dragon knots, looking rather white and scared. But as soon as he saw Florizella, he whispered as softly as he could:

"Florizella! Untie me, quick!"

Florizella had a look at the knots as she jumped out of the saddle and thought it would take her all of the forty-eight hours to get one of them undone.

"This is no time to save string," she said, and taking out her dagger she cut through the rope. She and Bennett were just about to get up on Jellybean and gallop away, when . . .

. . . the Dragon Woke Up!

As soon as the dragon saw Florizella
and Bennett, he let out a dreadful
great roar. His yellow eyes flashed,
and smoke spouted from both his
noses.

Florizella and Bennett went back to
back without saying a word, and both

drew their swords. The dragon lurched towards them, his two great scaly heads getting closer and closer. Florizella's sword went up, and Bennett's too, and before the dragon had a chance to blow flaming breath all over them, the two heroes brought their swords down with a mighty *swoosh* and a horrid *thwack* which resounded through the forest!

The dragon lay dead at their feet, disappearing from its toes up, as dragons do when their heads are cut off, and That was the End of Him, All Right.

"Yikes!" said Bennett. They both leaned down and wiped the blades of their swords on the grass and the ferns of the forest. Their swords were

smeared with the dragon's bright-green blood. It made them both feel a bit sick just to see it. When their swords were clean, they gave each other a good, hard hug and slumped down together in the grass and waited to get their breath back before riding home.

"You shouldn't have done it, though, Florizella," said Bennett, as they sat under the pine trees.

Florizella thought he was being polite.

"That's all right," she said, nicely. "I know you'd do the same for me."

Bennett wasn't being nice at all. He was being horrid, though he didn't mean to be and though he didn't know it yet.

"I'd do it for you," he said, carefully, "but you shouldn't have done it for me, because it's not how a Princess should behave."

Florizella stopped staring at the sky and listening to her heart, which was beating too fast because she had been so scared by the dragon. She took the stem of grass she was chewing out of her mouth, and she looked at Bennett. She did not look at him affectionately. She looked as if she thought that Bennett was about to say something stupid.

She was dead right.

"It's the Prince's job to do the rescuing," Bennett said. "Everybody knows that the Princess has to be caught by the dragon so the Prince can come along and rescue her. Then he asks her to marry him and they get married to universal rejoicing. Everyone knows that. That's how we should have done it."

"It wouldn't be universal rejoicing if we got married," Florizella said, nastily. "Because there would be one

person not rejoicing, and that would
be me. Of all the pompous boobies!"
She jumped up and whistled for

Jellybean and picked up the cut ropes and gathered up the swords in a very busy, cross way.

"That's how it's supposed to be done!" said Prince Bennett, a bit cross too.

Florizella put a hand on Jellybean's halter and looked at the Prince with blazing eyes.

"Suit yourself!" she said, crossly. "If you want to be best friends, then you come to me when I need you and I'll come to you when you need me. But if you want to be like other Princes and Princesses and get married as soon as something interesting happens, so that nothing interesting ever happens again, that's up to you! But I told you once and I'll tell you again. I *won't* get married yet, for a good long while. And I *won't* marry you just because we fought a dragon together. You said we were best friends, and that's what I want. But if you want to think of me as a Princess, then you can fight your own dragons . . . and I hope they eat you!"

And Florizella jumped on Jellybean, dug her heels in and scorched off at a gallop. She did not even look back at poor Prince Bennett, standing all alone in the Purple Forest with the dragon quite disappeared beside him.

She went home, put Jellybean back in his stall and gave him a rub-down and a feed. Then she climbed back up the ivy (for her bedroom door was still

locked) and pulled back the covers on
her bed, tumbled in and fell fast
asleep. She was very tired.

So she did not know until the next morning that she and Bennett were the best of friends after all. For when the rescue party arrived in the Purple Forest, he did not go straight home to where his parents were anxiously waiting. He rode all the way back to Florizella's Kingdom and, for the second time that day, he sought and found the King, Florizella's father.

He told him straight that he would not marry Florizella unless one day she really wanted to marry him.

"And I think, Sire," he said, "that a girl who is big enough to kill her own dragon is big enough to make up her own mind about getting married."

The King could not help but agree and give Prince Bennett a hug. And

the Queen, who had taught Florizella
sword-fighting in the first place,
nodded rather proudly and said:

"Well, Florizella was never quite an
ordinary Princess."

She hugged Prince Bennett too, and they sent him home in the second-best royal carriage, the silver one with the blue cushions. And from that day onwards no one *ever* suggested that the Princess Florizella should get married.

Least of all Prince Bennett.

OCHRE PARK IMC